Harry is curious about what he just heard so he gets up to peek outside.

Harry and his buddy go for a closer look. On the side of the road they find a long, skinny bag.

Harry knows the right thing to do is to find its owner. He lifts it on his shoulder and he and Ollie start back home.

Harry sets the long bag down. The book is an owner's manual.

Harry can hardly stop reading long enough to get the glider all the way home.

Harry calls up SkyHigh Gliders. For his honesty, they give him flying lessons. As fate would have it, there is a certified hang gliding school nearby. He can start next weekend. SkyHigh tells him to prepare by reading all the manual and practice setting up the Red Tail.

Harry knows that with training he can learn to be a hang glider pilot. After reading all the instructions, he can hardly wait to get the Red Tail out of its bag!

There are 12 battens that go in Red's sail to give it shape. Hmmm...

...Oh. HEY GUYS! I'm going to learn to fly! What do you think?

1) Sail
2) Nose
3) Leading edge
4) Trailing edge
5) Keel
6) Control Bar
   a)downtubes
   b)basetube

7) Hang straps
8) Wires
   a) nose wires
   b) side wires
   c) rear wires
   d) top wires
9) Battens
10) Kingpost
11) Tips

There are several steps to setting up the Red Tail. With practice, Harry will be able to "*set up*" or "*break down*" the glider in 15 minutes. When it's just about set up, a crowd begins to gather...

Harry starts training on flat ground again. But today, he will be hooked in the glider.

All of yesterday's practice begins to pay off as Harry's feet leave the ground for a brief moment.

Order Form

To order additional copies of Harry and the Hang Glider, please send check or money order to:

SkyHigh Publishing
201 N. Tyndall
Tucson, AZ 85719
USA

Enclose: $24.95(US) for each book $_____

Sales Tax: Arizona residents
          please add 6.75% $_____

Shipping: $4.95(US) for the first book and
          $1.50 for each additional book $_____

                                            _____

Total: $_____

(Please allow four to six weeks for shipping.)

Order Form

To order additional copies of Harry and the Hang Glider, please send check or money order to:

SkyHigh Publishing
201 N. Tyndall
Tucson, AZ 85719
USA

Enclose: $24.95(US) for each book $_____

Sales Tax: Arizona residents
          please add 6.75% $_____

Shipping: $4.95(US) for the first book and
          $1.50 for each additional book $_____

                                            _____

Total: $_____

(Please allow four to six weeks for shipping.)